When a Hero Dies
by Anne Schraff

Perfection Learning® Corporation
Logan, Iowa 51546

For information, contact:
Perfection Learning® Corporation
1000 North Second Avenue, P.O. Box 500,
Logan, Iowa 51546-0500.
Phone: 1-800-831-4190 • Fax: 1-800-543-2745
perfectionlearning.com

Paperback
ISBN-10: 0-7891-7549-5
ISBN-13: 978-0-7891-7549-6

Reinforced Library Binding
ISBN-10: 0-7569-8389-4
ISBN-13: 978-0-7569-8389-5

26816
7 8 9 10 11 12 PP 18 17 16 15 14

1 IT WAS THE most terrible day of Tony Gibbs' life.

It was worse than the day they moved from the nice house in Alabama. They'd left behind the moss-draped trees and the camellias around the front door to come to this crowded, smoky city.

It was even worse than the day his father left. Tony was only six then. It hadn't mattered much in the long run. Even when his father had lived with them, he wasn't home much.

No, this was the most terrible day of Tony's life. Somebody had just killed his best friend. Somebody had killed Hiram W. Jefferson, the tall mahogany-skinned man who ran the corner grocery.

Tony had heard about it just this morning. The news had hit him like a bullet.

Now, in stunned pain, he walked to school. It had been his own decision to go. He didn't want to stop and think about the horror of Mr. Jefferson's murder. Not with his heart aching as though someone had drilled a hole in his chest.

Michelle Calder walked alongside of Tony. "Was it robbery or what?" she asked.

"Robbery, I guess," Tony said. His throat was dry. It hurt to talk about it. Talking made it brand new and fresh like a raw, red wound.

"He had that little market for a long time, huh?" Michelle said. To Michelle it was just a sad thing. One of those stories you read in the papers. Poor elderly man, seventy years old, killed on the street. A blow to the head. Blood running onto the asphalt.

But to Tony it was the death of the man who was his true father. He wasn't related to Mr. Jefferson, not by blood. But that tall, straight-shouldered man taught Tony how to ride a two-wheel bicycle and shoot baskets.

And as Tony found his talent for running, Mr. Jefferson had been there. Almost every morning Tony practiced for the track meets with Mr. Jefferson looking on. Just the two of them—Tony running

around the football field, Mr. Jefferson
with his stopwatch.

"Shaved a second, m'boy," Mr. Jefferson
would say.

Tony would toss him a grin in return.

"You'll get to the Olympics someday,
Tony."

That was the dream they shared. Only
Mr. Jefferson and Tony really believed it.

"You liked him a lot, huh, Tony?"
Michelle asked.

Tony turned and looked at the girl. How
fine she was, like black porcelain. She
wore a short Afro and her eyes shone like
dark gold topaz. She and Tony weren't
going together, but maybe someday they
would.

"Michelle, he was my hero."

"It's really a shame people have to
do things like that. Mama says it wasn't
always like that around here. Not in the
old days," Michelle said.

"Yeah, this used to be a nice
neighborhood. Mr. Jefferson told me
everybody went to church. Folks came
out on warm nights just to talk and hang

around. Nobody was scared then. Now at night only the bad ones come out. It's like they own it all."

"Half the time, they don't even come to school. Like Zenza Dunne and Wayman Townes. Then when they do come to class, they just mess around. I wouldn't put it past guys like that to knock over a store and hurt some old man."

Tony felt the skin on the back of his neck crawl. If he actually knew who had killed Mr. Jefferson, he was afraid of what he'd do.

They reached the entrance to Adams High and Michelle turned to him. She lightly touched Tony's arm and said, "See you at lunchtime. I'm sorry, Tony. There's just so much hurt in your eyes. I'm real sorry."

Tony tried to smile, but he couldn't. "Saturday, this Saturday, we were—uh, we were going over to the school and I was gonna run. He was—I mean he had this new stopwatch. He got it just for that. Well, anyway—" Tony turned and hurried to homeroom.

Tony settled in a desk and stared glumly at his homeroom teacher, Mr. Bruce Campbell. He was also Tony's history teacher.

Mr. Campbell was always saying how good life could be. But he never had to deal with Mr. Jefferson's neighborhood because he didn't live near school. He drove his little black sports car from a nice suburb every day. He constantly bragged how he and his white, Asian, and Hispanic neighbors were like one happy family, fighting crabgrass instead of crime.

It was obvious Mr. Campbell felt he'd escaped from some terrible fate. And he pushed the kids as if he wanted each one of them to escape the same way he did.

"Education, education, and more education," he would bellow. "That's the ticket out of here."

The arrival of Andre Calder, Michelle's brother, shook Tony from his thoughts. Andre sat down next to him and said, "Man, we got that dog of a history test today. You study much, Tony? I didn't."

Tony stared at Andre. Why was he carrying on about a stupid history test? Who cared who won the Battle of Bull Run when Mr. Jefferson would never time another race? When he'd never again cheer Tony on or listen to his dreams and fears?

"Oh, hey man," Andre said, remembering. "Sorry, I forgot. You were close with that old grocer—"

"He wasn't 'that old grocer,' Andre. He had a name, you know? It was Hiram W. Jefferson."

"Yeah, right. That's really too bad. But you know, plenty people warned him not to stay open so late. But that old man, he was stubborn. How old was he anyway? Eighty?"

Tony slammed his history book shut. "It don't matter, Andre. He's dead!"

Tony didn't want to talk to anybody just then, not even Andre. Normally he and Andre got along fine. They had a lot in common—for instance, both were into sports. While Tony ran track, Andre was a star on the football team.

Being on the team always put Andre under heavy pressure. He had to keep a C average or get cut. He faced pressure at home, too. Andre's parents were hardworking, ambitious people who intended to make sure both their children were successful.

Now and again Andre would complain about how tough his life was. Most of the time Tony was willing to listen. But not this morning.

The homeroom bell rang and announcements began. A few minutes later, Wayman and Zenza swaggered in, late as usual.

Mr. Campbell hassled them, as he always did. But they didn't seem to mind. It was like a play. Everybody had lines to say. Nothing really changed from one day to the next.

After homeroom Tony went to history class. Mr. Campbell passed out the tests. Though his mind wasn't on the subject, Tony completed the test without much trouble. He wasn't unusually bright, but he knew how to study.

"You're nobody's fool, Tony," Mr. Jefferson used to say with a grin. "You take notes, you study, and you run like the wind. It's a gift, m'boy. It's a gift from God."

The memory brought tears to Tony's eyes, and he blinked angrily. He didn't want to cry.

When he finished the test, he walked to Mr. Campbell's desk and angrily slapped his paper on top. The teacher looked up in surprise. "Something wrong, Gibbs?"

"Nothin'!" Tony snapped back. "Everything's cool as can be, Mr. Campbell."

The teacher frowned. "Hang on, Gibbs. I'll see you after class."

Tony returned to his desk, slumped in his seat, and waited for the bell. Great, Tony thought bitterly. Now he'd riled up Campbell.

Tony honestly hadn't meant to smart-mouth the guy. Mr. Campbell was an okay teacher when he wasn't preaching at his classes. He honestly believed in what he told students—that education was the only way to succeed. He himself was going to school part-time getting his Ph.D.

Many parents thought Mr. Campbell was great, including Tony's mom. "You kids are so lucky to have that wonderful man teaching you," Mrs. Gibbs would say. "Tony, if your father had been half the man Mr. Campbell is, I can't tell you how different this family's luck woulda been!"

At last the bell rang. Up to the last minute Andre was still working furiously, sweat shining on his brow. But, like everyone else, he packed up his books when Mr. Campbell called for the tests.

As Zenza Dunne passed Tony's desk, he paused. "You in trouble, boy?" he asked, giving Tony's foot a kick.

Wayman Townes laughed. "He gonna get lectured by Mr. Campbell for having a sassy mouth."

Tony ignored them. Then when everybody had cleared out of the room, he went up to the teacher's desk. Before Mr. Campbell could say anything, Tony said, "Hey, I'm sorry I was—you know, rude. I've got some things on my mind."

Mr. Campbell looked him in the eye. "Gibbs, what bothers me is, you're not like the others. I'm used to them wising off. But when a good kid starts doing it, it makes me real depressed. You get my feeling? What's the problem? Is it something I can help you with?"

"No, Mr. Campbell, I don't think anybody can. You know Mr. Jefferson got killed, don't you?"

"Who? Oh, yeah. I heard something about that. A drug deal gone sour and he was caught in the crossfire. I heard it on the radio." Mr. Campbell shook his head.

Tony felt his cheeks go warm, then hot. "No, Mr. Campbell, it was nothing like that. Mr. Jefferson was a grocer, a very fine gentleman. Somebody just knocked him over the head, and he hit the curb and—and died."

"Oh. That's a shame. Did you know him well?"

Tony didn't know quite how to put it. He wanted to say, "This man was my grandfather, my father, my big brother. He was my teacher, my coach, my hero.

He was the only one I knew on this cold earth who would get up at five on a rainy day to watch me run. He was the rail-thin old man with the white hair and the white moustache who'd be clapping every time I ran. Didn't you ever hear the sound of those two strong old hands clapping, Mr. Campbell? Of course not. You don't live here."

But out loud, Tony simply said, "Yeah, I was close to him."

"It's ugly, Gibbs, and it's a shame, but that's what happens in neighborhoods like this. That's why I'm trying to help you kids get out of here. I know the way. I'm saying, hey, I was in a place like this myself—worse even. And I got out. There's a bigger, better world out there, and you can be a part of it!"

"Yeah, Mr. Campbell," Tony said. He wasn't in the mood for another pep talk, but he kept his irritation hidden.

The teacher glanced at Tony's test lying on his desk. He smiled.

"Look at your first few answers. All correct. You can be one of the success stories around here. You have what it takes, like I did."

"Uh—his funeral is tomorrow, Mr. Campbell."

"Whose funeral? Oh, the old grocer. I see."

"He was a good man, Mr. Campbell. He gave people credit when nobody else did. On their grocery bills, you know. And he always got good food in his market. He'd be down at the wholesaler early in the morning, making sure he got our share of nice, fresh vegetables. Not the kind of garbage most stores around here sell.

"And he kept the place clean. I'd go over and help him mop up. He always wanted it looking sharp. You don't see many clean stores like that around here, Mr. Campbell."

The teacher shook his head. "It's too bad he couldn't get to a better neighborhood where he'd have been safe."

"Oh, he could've, Mr. Campbell. He could've. He just didn't want to. This was his home. He belonged here. He said if everybody who's any good leaves, then the neighborhood will rot."

Tony turned and walked slowly from the classroom. He stopped at the door and repeated, "The funeral is tomorrow at the church on the corner."

* * *

The next day, Tony's mother was too tired to go to the funeral. Tony didn't blame her. She worked hard at the post office, sorting mail. She'd always say, "Mail's getting heavier all the time, and my back's getting older."

But Tony's eleven-year-old sister, Shauna, wanted to come. Mr. Jefferson had always given her a free apple or piece of candy. So Tony and Shauna walked down to the church together.

Tony thought Mr. Jefferson would have been pleased with the service. The choir was very good, singing Mr. Jefferson right across the Jordan. Most of the choir members had shopped in Mr. Jefferson's market. Now even as they sang, many of them were crying.

Little Shauna sang the loudest. She wanted to be a singer. She surely had the lungs for it, Tony thought. She could wail out a song to break your heart.

Almost all of the mourners were adults. But there was one little boy whose face Tony couldn't see. From the boy's mismatched clothing, he might've been Reggie Dunne, Zenza's little brother.

Soroya Curtis was the only one from Tony's class who came. She was an ordinary-looking girl. But when she smiled, she lit up a room.

Tony sat stonily during the service, only saying "Amen" once. And that was when the minister said Mr. Jefferson was surely in heaven.

"Look," Soroya said to Tony after the funeral. "Mr. Campbell sent these pretty red flowers. That was nice."

"Yeah," Tony said.

"He's the only person who sent flowers from the florist," Soroya said.

The other flowers were pathetic little bunches tied with homemade ribbons. Though they looked shabby, Tony liked them better than the ones from the florist. They came from people's hearts.

After the service, Tony, Shauna, and Soroya walked home together.

"Mr. Jefferson liked Tony best of anybody," Shauna said loudly. She usually spoke in a loud voice that reflected her lively personality. "You can ask anybody. He thought my brother was somebody real special."

"Yeah, I know that," Soroya said. "My mama said Mr. Jefferson always wanted a son, too. Maybe he kinda adopted Tony."

Tony remembered that Mr. Jefferson had talked now and again about his two daughters. One lived in Los Angeles, one in Houston. They were both thoughtful women who wrote and phoned their father frequently. Yet they rarely could spare the time to visit their father. He wondered if they had been among the mourners at the funeral.

"Tony was a lot like Mr. Jefferson's son," Shauna continued, proudly. "He told me last week that when Tony won the gold medal in the Olympics, he was gonna hang the medal in his store for a week. He said Tony already promised he could."

"If I'd ever made it there, I woulda kept that promise, too," Tony said.

"Do the police know anything about who killed him yet, Tony?" Soroya asked.

Tony stuck his hands in his pockets and shook his head.

"Just another murder, huh?" Soroya sighed. "I hate that stuff so much. My dad says he's gonna get us a gun, and Lord help any dude busting in our house. But that scares me, too."

"Lord help the dude that killed Mr. Jefferson," Tony said. Sudden anger boiled in him. His hands balled into tight, hard fists. They struck his muscular thighs like hammers.

Shauna looked up at her brother, her eyes wide. "You gonna get him, Tony? Make him pay for it?"

Soroya stopped walking. She grabbed Tony's hand and turned him around. "Tony Gibbs, don't go butting your nose into this. You leave it to the cops."

Tony looked at the girl. She was only fifteen, but she had eyes that went right to your heart.

Tony squeezed her gentle hand and smiled at her. Then he turned and ran up the steps to his family's apartment.

He hadn't said a word—he couldn't. The truth was, he wouldn't rest until Mr. Jefferson's murderer had been found.

2 BEFORE IT GOT dark, Tony jogged around the block. There was something about running that made him feel better. If he was happy, it made him happier. If he was sad, he could usually run the pain out.

"Hey, Tony." A familiar voice caught him as he rounded a corner.

"Hi, Andre," Tony said.

As Andre hurried near, Tony saw that his face was tense. "Tony, I'm in big trouble," Andre confessed.

"What's the matter? You're not still worrying about how you did on that test, are you?"

"You don't understand! I flunked, man! And if I flunk history, I'm off the football team. I'm not gonna get a chance for a football scholarship. I might as well be dead, man!"

"What're you talking about? How can you be sure you flunked? Even if you didn't do so great, Campbell's fair. He'll give you a chance to make it up. You know Coach Lansing's gonna have a fit if Campbell flunks the star of the Bobcats. Don't sweat it, Andre!"

"No, no, you don't get it, Tony. I cheated, man! I went and cheated on that lousy test!"

"You cheated? What'd you go and do that for?"

"You know how Dwight Stokes always gets A's? Well, he sits right beside me. I—I copied off his answer sheet!" Andre's voice was shaking.

"Okay, you cheated. But you aced the test, man," Tony said. He was getting tired of the whole conversation and wished he could continue running.

"No, you still don't get it! Wayman just told me: Campbell tricked us. He thought somebody was going to cheat, so he gave each row a different test. Nobody had the same test as the next person. Now Campbell is gonna know I'm a cheat 'cause I'll have the same answers as Stokes, but to all different questions! That cockroach Campbell!"

"Well, go to Campbell and admit you messed up," Tony said. "Tell him you're sorry."

Andre leaned against the storefront of the deli, rolling his eyes. "Right, he's gonna buy that one. Man, I could strangle that creep Campbell! Do you know he could ruin my whole life? He could be the difference between me going to college— playing pro ball and being rich—or just being a lousy wino."

Tony shook his head. "Hey, Andre, he's not my favorite guy either. But he didn't tell you to cheat, did he?"

"Yeah, what do *you* care? You've got school and sports licked," Andre said bitterly. "Now you got my sister eating out of your hand, too. You got the best-looking girl in school!"

"I haven't *got* Michelle, Andre. We're not going together. Hey, look, go see Campbell. Be up front with the man. He'll listen. See you later."

Tony quickly broke into a jog and left Andre behind. As he circled the block, he tried to put all thoughts out of his head. But he couldn't. When he passed Mr. Jefferson's market, he had to turn and look at it. He couldn't help it. It was like being a kid and trying not to look at the dark at the bottom of the stairs. You just have to look.

Tony stared at the little market, now so dark and empty. He could almost see the white head bobbing in there. He could almost imagine him carrying out a box of oranges, each one perfect. He always checked to get rid of the bad ones.

Out of the sky came the warm, rich voice. "Hey, gold medalist, you just shaved a second off your time."

Tony broke into a run as tears flew down his cheeks.

At the end of his workout, he stopped at a grocery store and bought a carton of orange juice. When he came out, he found Zenza standing there along with some friends.

"You still running in the track meet next week?" Zenza called to him. Tony didn't answer right away. "Hey, dummy. I'm talking to you." Zenza's buddies laughed.

Tony calmly drank some orange juice, then looked Zenza in the eye. "My name is Tony Gibbs. When you talk to me, use my name if you expect an answer. And, yeah, I'm running. And I'm winning."

They all laughed again. Zenza said, "That old man won't be pumping you up anymore. So maybe you won't run so fast."

"Yeah," one of Zenza's gang said, "he was your lucky charm. Now he's gone."

"Shut up!" Tony said with such ferocity that Zenza backed away.

Zenza looked around for support. Then he grinned, and said, "I'm taking Michelle Calder out one of these fine days, Gibbs. What you think of that?"

"I think you've fried your brain, man," Tony snapped. He turned and jogged home.

Tony couldn't remember a time when he hadn't been at war with Zenza. In grade school Zenza had been the biggest kid. That gave him power. He could grab your lunch, your new notebook, or anything. If he wanted the basketball you were playing with, he never asked. He just gave you a shove and took it.

But by the sixth grade, Tony got his burst of growth and it all changed. Nobody pushed Tony around anymore.

Nevertheless, the bad feelings just went on from year to year. When it turned out the two best runners at Adams were Tony and Zenza, things just got worse. Tony always left Zenza in his dust. He left everybody in the dust.

After every race, Zenza would grit his teeth in rage. But Mr. Jefferson, how his face would glow! "When I see you run, I see Kip Keino," Mr. Jefferson would say. What eyes he had, what a face! He could look wild with joy at happy times and crumpled in sorrow at sad times.

Tony stopped again and leaned his forehead against the window of a dry cleaning store.

Angrily he muttered, "Man, why did it happen? You shouldn't have left me, you know? Not you, not Mr. Hiram W. Jefferson. I needed you. You were—you were my hero. I mean, when a hero dies, what do you have left?"

Tears ran down his face, but this time he didn't try to stop them. He looked down the street. Through the growing darkness he saw the neon signs, "Liquor," "Whisky," "Bar." But one neon sign wasn't lit anymore. Its dark letters read "Market."

Tony stiffened. His hands turned into fists again. Whoever killed Mr. Jefferson had better not be out tonight.

Then he laughed bitterly at himself. Who did he think he was? Why, he was as crazy as his kid sister, thinking he could play detective and catch the killer.

But he couldn't shake the thought that somebody from around here had probably done it. Somebody had killed Mr. Jefferson. Now that somebody was sipping beer from a cool glass, or smoking dope, or laughing with a pretty girl on his arm. He was breathing the night air and watching the moon rise high in the sky. He didn't care what he'd done.

Maybe the killer didn't even know Mr. Jefferson well enough to say hello. He didn't know anything about the man he'd murdered.

Yet there was so much to tell. Hiram W. Jefferson, born in Tougaloo, Alabama. Started factory work by the time he was eleven. Fought in World War II and won medals for bravery under fire. Raised a family, ran a business. And changed the life of a lonely little boy named Tony Gibbs.

That familiar voice drifted into Tony's mind. "Hey, Tony, you gonna wink at me when they put that medal round your neck? Listen up, m'boy, I won't care if it's the bronze, silver, or gold. I kinda figure though that it just might be the gold."

Those words seemed cruel now. Who cared, Tony thought to himself. Maybe he'd win some stupid track meet, but he'd never get to the Olympics. No way. He was running his legs off for nothing.

Tony slowly walked the rest of the way home. As he entered the apartment, he heard Shauna wailing away from the bedroom.

Ah'm gonna love youuuu, babeee,
and you'll love me toooo.

*Got nothin' goin', sweet child,
'cept for this me and youuuu—*

Tony's mother smiled wearily and nodded in the direction of the bedroom. "That child is cra—zy. She'd do better reading her school books. She has 'bout as much chance being a singer as I have being president."

"Mama, she's getting good grades. Got lots of friends at school."

"Well, I just hate to see her heart set on foolish dreams. She reminds me too much of your father and his foolish dreams." She shook her head. "If he'd just done like Mr. Calder—worked at a regular job—it'd been so much better."

"Yeah, Mama," Tony agreed, but he really wasn't listening anymore. She always said the same things, over and over. Tony knew it by heart. He didn't even have to listen. He just had to say "Yeah, Mama," and it fit whatever she was saying.

***

At school on Monday, Michelle Calder came in sporting a beautiful ruby necklace. Her friends gathered around to admire it. It wasn't just a cheap thing. It had obviously cost some money.

"Where'd you get it, Michelle?" a girl asked in an awed voice. "Did your parents give it to you?"

Michelle laughed. "Oh, you gotta be joking. My parents would never spend money on something that wasn't absolutely necessary. Every penny they make they put away. No, this was a gift for my sixteenth birthday from Zenza Dunne!"

Tony turned sharply and stared. Michelle was spinning around, showing off. "That big, tough dude went and turned sweet on me, you guys!" she said with a laugh.

Tony wondered how Michelle could be so stupid. Zenza couldn't afford anything like that. The Dunnes had five kids and they knew every way possible to stretch meatloaf. Zenza didn't have a regular job either.

"Hey, Michelle," Tony snapped, "how you figure Zenza got the money for a thing like that?"

Michelle looked hurt. "Tony, don't be mean. Zenza does odd jobs. He's probably been saving. Don't spoil it for me. You know my parents give me nothing to spend on myself. It doesn't seem fair that I never get to wear anything beautiful. Zenza just handed it to me and said 'Happy birthday, babe,' and that was it. I think it was nice!"

When Zenza entered homeroom that morning, he grinned at Tony before taking his usual place in the back. It was a taunt. He'd shown Tony just how he intended to get Michelle's attention.

Tony sat back, boiling mad. He liked Michelle. He cared what happened to her. Michelle and Andre had been his friends as long as he could remember. He didn't want the girl wearing a piece of stolen jewelry!

And something else: it was just that ugly Zenza was trying to buy Michelle. Zenza knew she'd never really liked him that much. But he also knew how starved Michelle was for beautiful things.

After homeroom, Tony followed Zenza and stopped him. "Hey, man, where you coming from anyway? You stole that necklace, didn't you?"

Zenza glared at him. "One of these fine days, Gibbs, I'm gonna give you a mouthful of your own teeth. They're gonna be rattling around in your head like dice," he threatened.

Then he laughed and shook his head. "Michelle is one beautiful babe. She's got the right to pretty things. You ever see those old ladies in the paper, just hanging with jewels? It ain't fair for a girl like Michelle to have nothing but charms from a cereal box! Now she's got something she can show off, and it's from old Zenza!"

"You ripped it off, Zenza. How else would you get it?"

"You don't know nothin', Gibbs. You think you're so smart, man, but you don't know nothin'!"

"Where did you get it if you didn't rip it off? You don't work. Your folks even have trouble keeping food on the table," Tony said.

"You my warden, man? Did I get arrested and put in the joint? You just

mind your own business, Gibbs. I got ways
of making a little on the side."

A terrible, cold feeling gripped Tony. He
suddenly remembered: Mr. Jefferson had
been robbed of about two hundred dollars.
That was the amount he had written in the
cash register that day.

Somebody could buy a nice ruby
necklace for less than that. The rubies
wouldn't be first-class of course, but it
would be a showy piece of jewelry for a
sixteen-year-old girl.

Somebody who wouldn't mind hitting an
old man over the head could have pocketed
two hundred easy that way—Tony backed
Zenza into a corner. "Dunne, did you rob
Mr. Jefferson? Were you the one who stole
his money and murdered him?"

Zenza didn't back down. He just sneered
and said, "Don't pin that one on me, Gibbs.
Find some scared little wet-nosed kid. But
not me."

"If I find out you did, I'll get you, Dunne.
You can count on it," Tony said.

"You playing cop now, Gibbs?" Zenza
laughed.

"There's no hole dark enough for you to hide in if you did it, man," Tony said.

Zenza pulled away from Tony, still laughing. Across the hall, Michelle was showing somebody else her ruby necklace. Zenza hurried to join her.

Tony turned and stalked angrily away. But he couldn't get away before he heard Zenza crow, "Baby, you shine so fine!"

Tony could barely swallow his anger. After so many years, it looked like Zenza was again winning their private war.

3 ANDRE WAS FINISHING his talk with Mr. Campbell when Tony came in. From Andre's face, Tony could see the verdict. Mr. Campbell had no use for cheaters.

Andre slid into his desk, still shaking. "I got an F. That means I have to get a B on the next big test or I'm dead. I'm off the football team and everything. My folks are gonna chew me up one side and down the other. Man, I'm good as dead!"

Dwight Stokes, sitting in his usual place next to Andre, turned. "I saw you copying from me. I knew you were cutting your own throat."

Andre gasped. "Why didn't you *say* something?"

Dwight shrugged. "Never give a sucker an even break," he said.

Dwight was like that. He was the smartest kid in the junior class with a mind that worked like a computer. He gobbled up information, filed it, and spit it out whenever it was needed. But as far as people were concerned, he didn't seem to care if they existed.

"You lousy creep," Andre hissed at Dwight. "Someday I'm gonna get you."

Dwight laughed. "Stop breathing on me, rodent."

The bell rang and Mr. Campbell called the class to attention. "Today I'm going to show you a film about the revolutionary war. It may surprise you to learn that Black Americans took part in the war, too."

"But films never show that stuff," one girl objected.

"This one does. It's a special film I was fortunate to get. It stresses the role ethnic groups played in the Revolution."

"Oh Lordy, Mistuh Campbell," Wayman Townes mocked, "you all mean we's gonna see Cripo Attaturk shinin' George Washington's boots?"

"That's right, Townes, laugh it up. Play the big fool. But when you're scratching for a living because you didn't learn anything in school, the laughter will wear pretty thin." Mr. Campbell stared coolly at Wayman.

"Anyway, you haven't even got the man's name right." Mr. Campbell turned to the rest of the class. "Can anybody set Mr. Townes straight?"

"His name was Crispus Attucks, and he died during the Boston Massacre," Dwight Stokes said.

Mr. Campbell smiled gratefully at Dwight. Just when nothing seemed worth it, there was Dwight and his amazing fund of information.

Dwight was, without a doubt, Mr. Campbell's favorite student. His accomplishments were all the more striking because of his background. An abused child, he'd gone through a dozen foster homes. He'd never stayed long enough in any of them to become part of a family. Yet here he was—cool, smart, and making it.

Mr. Campbell started the film. As he had promised, it was unusual. It told the story of Peter Salem of the First Massachusetts Regiment who fought on Bunker Hill.

And of Oliver Cromwell who crossed the Delaware with Washington that cold, windy night in 1776. And, of course, it mentioned Crispus Attucks.

As they left class, Andre groaned. "All that stuff will be on our next test."

"I'll help you study, Andre," Tony promised. "Don't sweat it. But I'll tell you what you should be worrying about—that sister of yours. She got a necklace from Zenza. She's got to be crazy taking stuff from him."

Andre looked right at Tony. "You don't know how it is for us. Our parents make good money, but we eat hamburger stretched with oatmeal. We wear clothes from the thrift store. All our folks do is save money for the future. I don't blame Michelle for taking a gift like that."

"Even if it's stolen?" Tony asked. He wanted to add, "or bought with blood money—Mr. Jefferson's blood." But he stopped short of saying it.

"Tony," Andre said, "I don't know what's right and what's wrong. I just don't know. I know my old man will kill me if I screw up. Tonight both he and my mama will be waiting for me, asking if everything is okay at school. I'd have to be some kind of fool if I said no. But what if I flunk? They're gonna know, right?"

Tony thought it wasn't right for a father to threaten his kids. But then it wasn't right for a father to disappear like Tony's father did.

At home that night, Tony told his mother about Andre. "He's really scared of his father."

"Mr. Calder is a good man. He just wants what's best for his kids. I envy that Tessie Calder having such a reliable husband," Mrs. Gibbs said.

"He hits Andre, and Michelle, too, sometimes. I've seen him slap Andre right across the face. He's one mean man, Mama," Shauna said.

"Shut your mouth, girl. What do you know?" Mrs. Gibbs said, drying her hands after the dishes. Her hands were old-looking, though she was just thirty-five.

"You haven't got any idea what it's like trying to raise decent children in this world. Everything is against you. Most kids end up like that wild Zenza and the rest of those Dunne children. But that's 'cause all their mama does is party."

"Know what, Mama?" Shauna said. "Reggie Dunne told me that Mr. Calder ain't so mean. He says Dwight Stokes' father was twice as bad. He burned Dwight on the stove. He did it all the time. They had to put him in jail. Dwight's mama too, 'cause she never gave Dwight nothing but cornflakes."

"Shauna Gibbs, what did I tell you about talking to those Dunne children? They're nothing but trash."

Shauna shrugged. "Reggie is all right. He showed me his pigeons once."

The Dunnes—Tony was sick of the whole lot of them. He walked to the window and looked down the street. He could just barely see the corner where Mr. Jefferson died. It sent a fresh shudder through him.

He turned away from the window and spoke to his mother. "The track meet is Saturday, Mama."

"Well, good luck, honey. I can't go. I'm working Saturday."

"I know," Tony said. He didn't blame his mother for never coming to watch him run, even when she was off work. She didn't like sports. And she was tired; she was always tired.

But this would be the first time Tony would run without Mr. Jefferson being there. Mr. Jefferson had even come to a meet two weeks after his heart operation. Tony remembered thinking that the old man would stay home in bed. But the day of the race, there Mr. Jefferson had been in his usual place.

Tony took a deep breath and went to do his math. The one subject he hated was math. He took his book downstairs and sat on the front steps to try to do his homework. It was about that time Soroya came along.

"Hi, Tony." She peered at his book. "Math, huh? How's it coming? You need help?"

Tony smiled. Soroya was a math whiz. She always seemed to know when Tony needed help. Tony moved over on the steps and she sat down.

"Girl, you're too good to me," he said.

"Well, it's only because I love you, Tony Gibbs. I've loved you since the sixth grade. See how shameless I am?" She was laughing.

"You've always been my good friend, Soroya," Tony said.

She smiled. "Friend. Yeah, friend. But it's Michelle you're crazy about. I remember in sixth grade you gave her the prettiest valentine. And me—you gave me a funny one. I was so mad, I felt like tearing up that silly thing!"

"Did you?"

"No. Fool that I am, I kept it. I still have it." She laughed again.

"Know what, girl?" Tony said. "I got this equation and that equation and they're making me crazy—"

"Oh, it's not so bad, Tony. Let's just see." Soroya led him through the homework, making all the problems seem simple.

After they'd finished, Soroya asked, "You running Saturday?"

"Yeah."

"Oh good. I thought—"

"Yeah. He won't be there. First time. Gonna seem weird."

Soroya laid her soft hand on Tony's arm. "I believe he's gonna be there, Tony."

Tony couldn't answer for fear his voice would break. But he believed it, too.

"I wonder who did it," Soroya said quietly. "Couldn't have been somebody who knew him. He was such a kind man. He did something nice at one time or another for everybody I know. When my dad got laid off work just before Thanksgiving, Mr. Jefferson brought us a turkey and a whole bag of fixings."

"I believe it."

"Must have been a stranger killed him, Tony. Somebody who didn't know the kinda man he was," Soroya said.

Or somebody who didn't care, Tony thought to himself. He closed his eyes and saw Zenza's mocking face and then Michelle's necklace.

Tony turned to Soroya. "Did you see the necklace Zenza gave Michelle?"

"Sure, everybody in school saw it about five times. That girl pranced around like some old show dog."

Soroya's eyes suddenly widened. "Why? What's that supposed to mean, Tony?" She shook Tony's arm to make him speak. "What'd you mean?"

"What I mean is, where did Zenza all of a sudden get the money for that kinda thing?" Tony demanded.

Soroya shuddered. "You think Zenza robbed and killed Mr. Jefferson? Oh Tony, no! He got free apples and ice cream from Mr. Jefferson when he was growing up just like we did."

"He's never been any good, Soroya. Neither has Wayman or any of that gang. They were always ripping off little kids, stealing stuff in stores. I never saw Zenza go in a store he didn't take something without paying for it."

"But not killing, Tony. He couldn't have done that. None of *us* could have," Soroya insisted.

"Yeah, right. Just like that fine saying: 'the face of evil is the stranger's face.'

Well, maybe the evil one is right in front of us. We just never knew how bad he was."

Though she was upset, Soroya let the subject drop. They talked for a few minutes. Then, since it was getting dark, Tony walked Soroya home.

As they passed a closed dress shop, Soroya spotted a beautiful mannequin in the window. "Hey, Tony, look at that mannequin. Doesn't she look like Michelle? I wonder what it feels like to be so beautiful."

"Maybe being beautiful, you feel you got the right to nice things. Even if you don't," Tony snapped.

"Tony, it's just eating you up that Michelle is wearing a necklace Zenza gave her. It means Zenza cut in on your girl. That's what's making you so boiling mad. You're jealous!"

"No," Tony fumed. "You've got it all wrong. I don't grudge the girl a nice present. It's just that somebody robbed and killed Mr. Jefferson. Maybe that somebody used the money to buy a fine necklace!"

They reached her door. Before she went in, Soroya said, "Tony, don't be such a pig-headed fool. It was one of *them* that done it." She nodded at a dark sedan that was sliding by. "Or one of *them.*" She glared at two shadows slipping around the corner.

Tony recognized the figures almost without looking. Not by name or shape but by what they did. The men in the car had been making a drug deal with the shadows on the street. Had they come here to buy or sell? Who knew?

"Don't you see, Tony, they just come here to do crime and then they go."

"Where do they go, Soroya? Don't they live anywhere? Maybe they live on a street like this, and people figure they're okay because they're familiar."

Tony angrily shook his head. Then, with a sad wave to Soroya, he turned and strode toward home.

Tony figured plenty of people looking at him would label him as one of *them*, too. He was very tall for a sixteen-year-old boy. And his skin was deep black, not like Mr. Campbell's creamy brown.

Of course, he didn't dress fancy. He wore just a stocking cap—pulled down against the cold wind—a dark jacket, and jeans. But then some of the pushers and dealers didn't wear flashy clothes either.

Tony hurried down the street. He made up his mind that this time he wouldn't look at the empty market when he passed. But he ended up staring inside anyway. He imagined Mr. Jefferson putting big red apples in ruffled paper containers "because these folks need something pretty, too."

"Do you think somebody will open it up again?"

Tony looked up, startled. "Oh— Dwight. I didn't see you," he said. "Open it again? I don't know. It'll seem funny to see somebody else in there."

"It was real convenient," Dwight said. "The old lady sends me out for milk and stuff. Now I gotta walk twice as far."

"You talking about Mrs. Jensen?"

"Yeah."

"She's pretty good for a foster mom, isn't she, Dwight? I met her once at parents' night. She seemed okay," Tony commented.

"Ah, she'll sit in front of the TV watching her stupid game shows. Every once in a while, she yells, 'Dwight, run and get me some ice cream.' Or 'Dwight, run to the corner and get me a newspaper.' Like I'm her slave."

Dwight laughed bitterly. "She's just in it for the money. You should see her grab that county check when it comes."

"But isn't she using part of the money on you? I mean, she has to get paid, doesn't she?" Tony asked.

"*Has* to, is right. She can fall down a manhole for all I care," Dwight said. He looked into the dark market. "You were real tight with that old man, weren't you?"

"Yeah, yeah, I was. Say, you got any idea who might've killed him?"

Dwight was silent for a moment. Then he said casually, "Wayman Townes probably did it."

"Wayman? How come? What makes you say that?" Tony asked, his heart suddenly hammering.

"He's the kind of jerk who'd knock somebody over for a few bills."

"You got any proof, Dwight?"

"Just what I hear on the street, man." Dwight drew closer to Tony. "Say, how's Andre doing? He really messed up copying my answer sheet. I couldn't believe he'd be so stupid."

"Maybe you should've tipped him off. Sure would have saved him a lot of grief."

Dwight smiled. "That so? I s'pose that's what you'd have done, huh Tony? You're nice like that. You're nice to everybody. And everybody is nice to you. That's how life works for you, man. You get it, you give it. Like a gumball machine. Put the money in, get the gumball out."

Dwight squinted his eyes in a bitter expression. "Well, nobody ever put anything in my gumball machine. So I don't give out gumballs—or favors."

"Come on, man. Mrs. Jensen ain't so bad. And Mr. Campbell thinks you're the best thing in school."

"That rodent?" Dwight laughed. "Don't you just hate that slimy little preacher?"

Tony had had enough. But as he turned to go, Dwight said, "Oh, yeah. About what you said earlier. I've got proof about Wayman killing the old guy."

Tony spun around in an instant. "What?" he demanded.

"You know how Jefferson was always collecting stamps from Africa? Well, Wayman has one of those stamp books now. I bet he knocked off Jefferson and then stole it from the store."

The whole street began to spin like a giant Ferris wheel. The lights were making blurry orbits as Tony took off running.

4 WAYMAN TOWNES LIVED in an apartment four blocks over. But Tony would have gone any distance, no matter how late the hour. He ran the four blocks in a long, angry stride. At the apartment building he dashed up the stairs and pounded on the door.

A frightened-looking grandmother answered the door. "Mercy, I thought it was the police," she said. "What are you doing here? You're Missus Gibbs' boy, ain't you?"

"Yes ma'am. I need see Wayman."

"Well, come on in." She backed up, shouting, "Wayman, the Gibbs boy wants to see you."

Wayman came into the front room. "Well, if it ain't the ugliest dude on the street."

It was an old joke that went back to the time when Wayman and Tony had been friendlier to each other. The truth was, Wayman wasn't good-looking. Tony, on the other hand, was just about the handsomest boy in their crowd. So Wayman would call Tony ugly and everybody—including Tony—would laugh. But the laughing had ended some time ago.

"I need to see you alone, man!" Tony snapped.

"Am I getting busted or what?" Wayman asked in a mocking voice. He led Tony to the tiny room he shared with a brother. It was empty now.

"You got Mr. Jefferson's stamps?" Tony demanded.

"So what if I have?" Wayman yelled back.

"You stole them!" Tony cried.

"Are you crazy? No way! The old man had a stamp book he didn't like, so he gave it to me. So what? It was just a junky old thing. He was a crazy old man and—"

Tony grabbed Wayman's shirt front. "Shut your mouth!"

"Gibbs, you're one crazy dude! I'm telling you he gave me the lousy stamp book last year. He wanted to get me into this stamp collecting."

Wayman turned and dug in a pile of debris on the floor. He finally pulled out a large loose-leaf notebook. "Here, this is it!"

Tony felt numb. Wayman's words rang true. Mr. Jefferson had always been trying to get neighborhood kids into hobbies. It was even possible he'd been working on a lost cause like Wayman Townes.

Wayman hurled the book at Tony's feet. "Here, take it! I didn't want 'em when he gave 'em to me. I don't want 'em now. He was an old fool. What do I care about little colored bits of paper? You take 'em, Gibbs."

Wayman suddenly moved closer. "You take 'em and beat it out of here. Get moving, man, before I decide to beat the livin' daylights out of you."

Tony picked up the book. It fell open on a page with bold, bright stamps. One from the Kingdom of Burundi showed a big gray elephant trumpeting. Another, hailing from Nigeria, was a striking red stamp. Scrawled on the inside of the front cover were the words, "To Wayman Townes, on your fifteenth birthday. Your friend, Hiram W. Jefferson."

Tony laid the book down and left without a word.

* * *

On the morning of the track meet, Tony woke depressed. Usually on race days he felt a special excitement and the charge of his blood pumping strongly. But today the inside of his mouth felt like ashes and he had a headache.

Tony got dressed and was at the track at nine. Already quite a few people were in the bleachers. They were expecting a good meet. Four high schools would be competing with their best runners.

To the winner of each event went a great-looking trophy. Tony had made a nice, high shelf for it, opposite his bed. He planned to have the trophy be the first thing he saw each morning when he opened his eyes.

But it didn't matter so much anymore. Not without Mr. Jefferson there to share it with him.

Shauna sat in the front row with Soroya

and her brothers. Quite a few other kids from the junior and senior class at Adams were also there.

"Good luck," came Michelle's voice, soft as a feather. Tony turned to thank her. But then he saw she was looking at Zenza Dunne.

"I'm winning it for you, babe," Zenza said.

Michelle caught Tony's glance. She looked miserable for a minute. Then she smiled and said, "I hope the best guy wins, okay?" As she turned her head, Tony saw she was wearing a pair of lovely ruby earrings.

"Are those new earrings, Michelle?" he asked.

"They go with the necklace, birdbrain," Zenza snapped. "They ain't near good enough for a girl like Michelle."

For a moment Tony stared at Michelle's glowing red earrings and necklace. Then he looked at the spot in the bleachers where Mr. Jefferson used to sit. Red—the color of rubies and the color of blood.

It was time for his race. The runners

began to get on their marks for the sprint.

This was Tony's best event. He was a natural sprinter, the coach said. "Sprinters can't be trained. They're born, kid, and you got it!"

As they lined up, Zenza stepped close to Tony. "Hey," he whispered to Tony, "the old man ain't here. See, he ain't over there in the bleachers in his crazy hat with the feather on it. See that, man? Means you got the same chance as a snowball in hell of finishing first!"

Tony felt like pounding Zenza into the dirt and forgetting all about the race. But what good would that do?

Tony and Zenza slipped into place and tensely waited for the signal. Then came the gunshot, and they were off.

Tony ran with his long stride, knees high, arms pumping, leaning forward into the wind. That's the way he always got to the finish line ahead of everybody else.

But those other times he felt light, like he was flying. Now his legs felt like lead. Something was wrong.

Tony pushed himself to go faster. But

when he reached down for that burst of energy, he didn't have it. He watched in misery as Zenza streaked in front and crossed the finish line way ahead of him.

After the race, Soroya and Shauna tried to comfort him. "Don't feel bad," Soroya said. "Everybody has bad days."

"Yeah, you'll beat him next time," Shauna seconded.

"You just didn't have it today, kid. Too bad," the coach said. "But it's good that Adams won, right?"

Maybe, Tony thought, Mr. Jefferson was my lucky charm. Maybe suddenly I'm that six-year-old nothing again. Just the kid who couldn't ride a two-wheeler or even tie his shoes!

Andre came over and gave Tony a glass of water. "It feels like fumbling the ball at a game, huh?"

"Something like that."

Just then Zenza came up. "Want to see my trophy, Gibbs?" he gloated, waving it in Tony's face.

Tony knew the right thing to do would be to congratulate Zenza. That's what sports are all about, aren't they? Teaching you to be a graceful winner and a stylish loser.

But Tony couldn't make the words come out. He just turned his back and walked away with Shauna.

Soroya ran after the pair. "Okay if I walk home with you guys?"

"You better not. I'm feeling pretty rotten."

"Maybe I could cheer you up," Soroya said hopefully.

Tony turned, his voice sharper than he wanted it to be. "Not now, Soroya. I'm not in the mood to be cheered up. I know you're meaning well, but not now. Okay?"

Soroya fell behind, disappointed.

Tony strode quickly away. Shauna had to almost run to keep up. "Tony, you're hurting worse about Mr. Jefferson than you were when Daddy left, huh?"

"It wasn't nothing when Daddy left, Shauna. I didn't even know him. He was home maybe one day a month. Mr. Jefferson, I saw him every day. He—he thought sure I was something special."

"You are special, Tony. I'm real proud of you," Shauna said.

Tony stopped and looked at his little sister. Then he threw his arm around the girl's skinny shoulders and hugged her carelessly. "What do you know? You're just a crazy kid."

"You'll get to the Olympics, Tony. I just know it."

"Mama's right. It's all a bunch of garbage," Tony snarled.

"No it ain't. It ain't!" Shauna cried.

"Remember when Grandma came visiting from Alabama? She said Daddy dreamed all the time. She said his dreams were like little fires that never burned out. But Mama, she was always throwing water on Daddy's fires. Well, maybe she had to."

"No!" Shauna protested. "I love Mama, Tony. I truly do. But she oughtn't put out dream-fires."

***

Tony spent the rest of the weekend quietly, still numb with all his recent losses.

On Sunday, he studied with Andre. There was another history quiz coming up, and Andre was half-mad with worry.

"Seems like your folks should be more worried about Michelle dating a bum like Zenza than how you do in history," Tony said. "Don't they care about that?"

Andre laughed. "Man, are you a fool or what? They don't even know about Zenza."

"Well then, how's she explain the necklace and earrings?"

"She hides 'em when the folks are around."

Tony didn't say more about it, but a thought began to grow in his mind like a poisonous weed. He couldn't shake it.

After Andre left, Tony walked to the phone. He paused as he picked up the receiver. Never before in his life had he done a thing like this. He felt bad about doing it. It would surely get Michelle in big trouble.

But now, where there used to be pride and warmth in Tony's heart, there was little else but pain. He wanted to lash out at something, somebody.

It frustrated him that, as of yet, nobody had been arrested for Mr. Jefferson's murder. It was as if his old friend had dropped into a great sea. For a little while the waters churned, but now they were smooth again.

The grocery store—Mr. Jefferson's little kingdom—was being changed without protest, too. They were bringing in a new grocer next week. Prices would go up, quality down.

Tony had heard two neighbors talking about another change in the store just today.

"Hear they're going to be renting some of those adult movies," a man had said.

"Old Mr. Jefferson wouldn't rent 'em. Not even when some folks asked."

"Liquor too. They'll be selling that."

Tony remembered that Mr. Jefferson had vowed he'd never sell alcohol, despite the profit. "I'm not going to start selling lies to these people," he'd declared. But none of that mattered now.

Somebody had killed Mr. Jefferson. Somebody had killed the only gentle and beautiful thing on a street full of violence and despair. Tony thought it just might be Zenza who'd done it. And Zenza was buying whatever he wanted with that blood money, including Michelle.

Tony dialed the number. A woman answered.

"Mrs. Calder?" Tony said softly.

"Yes? Who is this?" Mrs. Calder was a cleaning woman. She had her own cleaning business with four employees. She sounded refined, like an uptown lady.

"Mrs. Calder, I'm a friend of Michelle's. I think you should know that she's dating Zenza Dunne. He gave her a real expensive ruby necklace and earrings. I just thought you should know."

Tony hung up. He felt guilty and dirty. Had he really done the right thing?

Tony didn't sleep much that night. He kept wondering what his phone call had done to Michelle. It was like shooting a gun at a target far away. You couldn't tell at that distance how much damage your bullet had done.

Tony kept telling himself he had done it for Michelle's sake. She was a nice girl. She deserved better than Zenza Dunne. Her parents, who'd sacrificed so much for their kids, deserved better, too.

But Tony knew deep in his heart he hadn't done it for Michelle. He had done it to ease his own hurt.

It never occurred to Tony that Michelle would know that he was the one who had made the call. But when he got to school the next morning, she was standing next to his locker waiting for him.

He saw she'd been crying. He also noticed that she wasn't wearing her ruby necklace and earrings.

"How could you?" Michelle asked in a shaky voice. "I know it was you, Tony. After what you've been saying to Andre. Don't try to deny it."

Tony didn't try to lie. He was no good at it anyway. "Your parents should know you're dating a hood like Zenza and taking stolen jewelry from him."

"You creep! Mama sent my beautiful jewelry back to the Dunnes! And Daddy whipped me with his belt until I cried! Are you glad? Did you want to see me hurt? Now I can't go out on weekends or after school or anything. You've ruined my whole life!"

"Ruined it?" Tony protested. "I'll tell you who would've ruined it: Zenza Dunne."

Fury flashed across Michelle's face. She flew at Tony and slapped his face as hard as she could. Tony rocked backwards, catching himself on the windowsill.

"You were jealous of Zenza and that's why you did it! That's all it was! You wanted me to date you. So when I dated Zenza, you had to get even!"

Michelle stepped back and glared at him. "You know what? I'm glad you lost that race! I hope you never win another race as long as you live! I wish you were dead and in the ground with old Hiram Jefferson!"

5 TONY HAD NEVER lost so many friends so fast. Everyone seemed to have heard what he did to Michelle. Everywhere he turned, people cut him cold.

Andre joined his accusers as well. In the hall between classes, he pulled Tony aside.

"You know what, man?" Andre said coldly. "Losing that grocer messed up your head. You built him into such a hero. But he wasn't, he really wasn't. Fact is, he was a mean old man. He stuck his nose into other people's business. I think that's why he's dead now.

"I never told you this before, Gibbs, 'cause you're so straight. But one time I tried to buy coke on the corner 'cross from his store. Old Jefferson saw me and called my folks. My old man came and got me. He whupped me so bad I couldn't sit down for a week."

Tony stared at Andre. "You were dumb

enough to try coke?"

"I just wanted to see what it was like. But old Jefferson ratted on me—just like you ratted on Michelle. I was so mad, I could've smashed in his skull. I thought, who does that old man think he is?"

Tony angrily retorted, "Maybe you *did* smash in his skull."

Andre couldn't believe it. "Man, you're out of your mind. I feel sorry for you. I surely wouldn't want to be you. Listen up, man. Everybody hates you for what you did to Michelle. Everybody hates you, Gibbs."

With that he left. Tony trudged on to class, feeling everyone's hostile glares.

Tony wasn't sure even Soroya would stick by him, but she did. At lunchtime she come over and sat beside him on the grass.

"I know you did a rotten thing, Tony. But I also know that you didn't do it to be mean and spiteful. You did it to help Michelle."

Tony gulped. It was tough to admit the truth to his only remaining friend. But he did. "No. I *did* do it to be mean and spiteful. Like Dwight says, 'When bad things happen to you, you want to make other people hurt too.' "

"Tony, that's just not like you. You're being real hard on yourself. Zenza's a rotten hood. Michelle shouldn't be hanging round with him."

Tony lay back on the stubble of grass and looked up at the sky. "I wish I could go someplace and run and run until I busted into little pieces."

* * *

The next few days were just as tough for Tony. Andre did well on the history test because he'd studied with Tony. But he wouldn't admit it. Like everyone else, he stayed away from Tony.

Zenza and Wayman were even rougher on Tony. They taunted and mocked him. They also trashed his locker twice, daring him to report it. Tony knew better than to say anything.

But Zenza's taunts were nothing compared to Michelle's coldness. She refused to even look at Tony. Tony watched in agony as she strolled past with Zenza. Now Michelle and Zenza were together almost all the time at school. Michelle couldn't go out with him, but they held hands and kissed all the time at school. Somehow Zenza had even managed to get back the ruby necklace and earrings for her to wear.

Zenza noticed Tony's watchful eye. He cornered Tony and warned what would happen if Michelle's parents received any other "crank calls."

He sneered and said, "That happens, Gibbs, *someone* just might catch you alone on a dark street and break both your legs."

Tony didn't believe Zenza. The threat wouldn't have stopped him anyway. But he didn't call Michelle's parents again. What good would it do? It had only made things a thousand times worse the first time.

Another painful sight was the reopened market. Tony made a point of walking on the other side of the street when he passed. But even from across the street he could see the crummy half-rotten oranges and brown bananas. And still nobody knew who'd killed Mr. Jefferson.

But daily the hurt inside Tony lessened, and the sharp pain turned dull. He felt numb.

Others saw the change in him, too. "You've stopped caring about everything," Shauna accused him as he let her win another word game.

"Quit nagging me, girl," Tony said.

"Won't you run anymore, either?"

"I don't know." There was another track meet in a couple weeks. Zenza would be running, and there would be strong competition from other schools, too. Tony wasn't sure if it mattered enough to even try.

Tony went for a walk one evening. As he prowled the noisy streets, he saw a convertible glide by. Zenza was driving, and Michelle was beside him.

Tony angrily shook his head. Mr. and Mrs. Calder were out of town for a funeral. Andre had promised to watch his sister, but Michelle could always get around him.

Tony kicked a crumpled milk carton into the gutter and just kept on walking.

As he passed the market, he thought briefly of Mr. Jefferson's old apartment in back of it. Whenever Tony had needed somebody to talk to, he'd just dropped in. Now there was nobody who really understood.

As Tony turned the corner, he heard a girl scream. The cry came from a brushy vacant lot where a furniture store once stood. The place had burned down a few years back. Now kids pulled in there on dates.

Tony had enough street-smarts not to mess in some fight between gangs. But this didn't sound like a clash over turf.

Then he spotted the back of Zenza's convertible. The scream came again— from the car. It was Michelle!

Tony hurtled toward the car and yanked the door open. "Leave her be!" he shouted.

"Keep your nose out of this, man," Zenza hissed back.

But Michelle immediately lunged out the door and stood trembling beside Tony.

She looked scared. But apart from having her clothes torn, she seemed unhurt.

Tony glared at Zenza. "Dunne, you're gonna wish you were never born if I tell Michelle's daddy what you tried to do! You put that car in gear and make tracks, man!"

At that, Zenza leaped out of the car, spitting curses. He came at Tony like a wild man. Tony blocked the attack, driving a hard fist into Zenza's midsection.

In all the years since Tony got his growth, there was never any question who was the strongest. Tony was a tough, hard-muscled athlete. Zenza was just a bully who could only get the best of smaller kids.

The fight was over in short order. Zenza ended up sitting in the brush, blood running from his split lip. He scowled at Tony with helpless hatred.

Tony didn't wait around for Zenza to get his strength or courage back. He grabbed Michelle's arm. "Come on," he said.

As Tony walked Michelle home, he asked if she wanted to file a complaint.

"I just want to go home and forget this ever happened!" she said, wiping tears from her face.

She said scarcely another word. Tony guessed that she was feeling both ashamed and angry. She obviously never thought Zenza would get so rough if he didn't get his way.

At her apartment door, Michelle paused and turned to Tony. "Please don't tell my parents about this, will you? My father would kill him—and maybe me, too."

"I won't tell anybody," Tony promised.

Michelle gave a weak smile of gratitude. Then she asked Tony to come in. Tony hesitated until he saw the plea in Michelle's eyes. He followed her in.

They found Andre sitting at the kitchen table, studying. When he saw Michelle's torn clothes and mussed hair, he jumped up. "Michelle, what happened? Are you all right?"

"I—it was Zenza. He wanted to show off this car he had. Next thing I knew, he was all over me. I don't know what would have happened if Tony hadn't come."

Andre looked sick. "Oh man! Oh man! You *promised* me you'd be okay with Zenza. You said nothing would happen!" He shook his sister. "Nothing happened, did it? I mean, you're okay, right?"

"Nothing happened!" Michelle screamed in Andre's face.

Andre released her, then turned away in disgust. "This is all I need! Don't I have enough to worry about? Why'd you go out with that dude? You're such a fool, Michelle! If anything had happened, you know who'd get the blame!"

Andre whirled around again. "That's the last time, girl! The last time you have anything to do with Zenza!"

Michelle bristled. "Don't order me about, Mister Calder!" Her voice softened. "Anyway, I don't mean to ever speak to Zenza Dunne again."

Andre growled and gathered up his books. He retreated to his bedroom and slammed the door.

Michelle sighed and then glanced at Tony. "You must hate me," she finally said.

Tony shook his head.

"Tony," she continued softly, "one time you offered me your school ring. I— I'd sure be proud to wear it now."

Tony looked at Michelle. She was still the most beautiful girl he'd ever known. But he was no longer the boy who had offered her his school ring. He would never be that boy again.

"I'm glad you're all right, Michelle," he said quietly, patting her hand. "You get some rest now. I gotta go home. Mama'll be worried if I'm much later. These are mean streets, especially at night."

Tears streamed down Michelle's cheeks.

***

With each passing day, Tony realized there was less chance that Mr. Jefferson's killer would ever be found. He'd heard that if a crime was going to be solved, it was generally within the first few days afterwards. Time was on the crook's side.

The murder was always at the back of his mind. But life forced Tony to think about other things—school, for example. In history class, Mr. Campbell continued to frustrate Andre by making more tough assignments.

That Monday, book reports were due. Mr. Campbell called the class to order and asked for the papers. "Hand 'em in, people. But don't everybody rush up at once." He laughed.

Dwight quickly handed over his report. It was bound in a red folder, all fifteen pages of it. Mr. Campbell had said the book reports must be a minimum of five pages. But he had set no upper limit.

"Well, well," Mr. Campbell said approvingly as he scanned Dwight's work. "Dwight's book report is on *two* books by John Hope Franklin. I just hope the rest of you were half as ambitious."

"What a freak!" Wayman snarled.

"I'm gonna drill a hole in your head and let your brains leak out, Stokes," Zenza whispered bitterly.

The two boys hadn't been quiet enough. Immediately Mr. Campbell called, "Townes, Dunne, you'll be glad to know you'll be on detention for the rest of this week! I hope that doesn't interfere with any of your after-school activities. If so, that's just too bad!"

The rest of the class seemed to drag on. When the bell finally rang, a girl turned to Dwight. "Why did you write so much?" she asked. "You made the rest of us look bad."

"I can't help it if you're stupid," Dwight said.

"Aw, come on, dude," Andre said, "this class is bad enough without you in it!"

"Stop breathing on me, rodent," Dwight said as he sauntered out.

"What's he trying to prove?" someone asked.

"He's not human," Wayman said. "Just a freak."

Tony wasn't interested in Wayman's troubles or Dwight's. He exited the room and set off for his next class. As he passed a couple of freshmen, he heard one say, "Hey, I like that market better than when the old man ran it. They got neat movies now and magazines, too!"

The other boy heartily agreed. "Yeah!

We get movies there, too. And the guy doesn't mind who he rents to—even kids!"

"Shut up, you little creeps," Tony snarled at the younger boys. "You don't know what you're talking about."

The pair of them got wide-eyed and fled. Tony was six feet tall, and he'd forgotten how he looked to a freshman.

Soroya had overheard the whole conversation. She came up and quietly said, "That's not like you, Tony. Where do you get off yelling at those poor kids?"

"Little creeps. Can't think of nothing but renting dirty movies!"

"Tony, I know that Mr. Jefferson meant a lot to you. But it's time to put this behind you. It's not right to keep thinking about it."

"But they haven't nailed his murderer yet. Man, they haven't even got a lead."

"Lot of crimes go unsolved. It's sad, but—"

Tony scowled at Soroya. "They've got to solve this one. They've got to! Every guy I look at, I'm thinking, 'Hey man, was it you?' "

"You know, there are places you could go to get help."

"Help? Help to catch the hood who did it? Or help with 'my' problem?"

He continued, "I know what you want, Soroya. You want me to see a head doctor and make myself feel good about Mr. Jefferson getting killed. Hear that it's okay somebody killed a great man and got away with it. Well, it's not okay. It's not ever going to be okay."

"But Tony—" Soroya pleaded.

Tony pounded his fist against a wall. Then he hurled his history book against a locker where it exploded open.

"No!" Tony shouted. "It's *not* okay that somebody killed Mr. Jefferson and got away with it! It isn't going to be that way!"

6 THE NEXT DAY after school, Tony went to the police station. He asked the desk sergeant for the name of the detective investigating Mr. Jefferson's murder.

At first the sergeant didn't seem to even recognize Mr. Jefferson's name. It was just as Tony feared. Nobody was working on the case anymore. The cops had forgotten it, just like everybody else!

But then a young lieutenant came over. He held out his hand to Tony. "I'm Lt. Askia Peters. You wanted to see me?"

"You the one working on Mr. Jefferson's murder?" Tony asked bluntly.

"Yes. What's your name?"

"Tony Gibbs."

The lieutenant motioned Tony into a chair. "Do you have some information that might help us, Tony?"

"No. It's just that—see, Mr. Jefferson was a friend, a really good friend. And—

well, it's been a month now, and no one's been arrested."

Lt. Peters nodded. "Well, we have a lot of crimes to investigate. Other murders, too. Your case is specially difficult because there're no witnesses and no real leads. We took prints from the cash box. But we need a suspect to match them with."

"Mr. Jefferson was real—special," Tony strained for the right word. He had to make this cop understand somebody *important* had been killed. Not that all people aren't important, but Mr. Jefferson really cared about his neighbors and friends.

Tony wanted to tell Lt. Peters about Mr. Jefferson. The cops should know how, if a kid was in trouble, Mr. Jefferson would be there to help. Or if a government check were late, he'd put a package of food at your door.

But Mr. Jefferson never wanted to embarrass people. When they'd catch him and thank him, he'd stomp off, almost angry.

Tony leaned forward, pleading with the cop to understand. "He was just about the greatest man I ever knew."

"Is that right?" said Lt. Peters. He looked sympathetic. "I'm sorry I didn't know him. But, you see, all that kindness wouldn't mean a thing to a sociopath. Sociopaths have no feelings. They rob, they kill—nothing matters to them. I'm afraid it was someone like that who killed Mr. Jefferson. It's a damn shame."

The lieutenant concluded by looking at his watch. He made it clear he was finished talking to Tony.

Tony stood up and mumbled thanks. Then he left the station, feeling worse than ever. It really was hopeless. They weren't looking for the killer anymore.

Tony didn't blame Lt. Peters. He seemed like a nice guy. But as he'd admitted, he just didn't know Mr. Jefferson. He saw him only once, lying in the street, blood streaming from his white thatch of hair. The lieutenant never heard Mr. Jefferson's rumbling laugh. He never saw the twinkle in his eyes or the warmth and courage in his soul.

Across the street from Mr. Jefferson's market, Tony sat down on the curb and bowed his head. He remembered sitting here about ten years ago on this street. He'd been trying to learn to ride a two-wheeler, without much success. Finally his mother, who had been trying to teach him, had sat him down.

"Child," she'd cried in frustration, "you just ain't any good at this. You can't do it. Listen, it's no crime not being able to ride a two-wheeler. You be satisfied with walking."

But Tony had wanted with all his heart to ride that two-wheeler. He tried again and fell again. At last his mother went inside and left him alone.

That was the day Tony first met Mr. Jefferson. The grocer had come out of his market and watched Tony for a time. Then he called out, "You can ride that bike, m'boy. You can if you make up your mind."

Tony tried and fell again. The grocer hurried over and helped Tony up. Then with a strong hand guiding the bike, he walked beside Tony. Tony pedaled away, slowly finding his balance.

All the while Mr. Jefferson gave Tony warm words of encouragement. Finally he smiled big. "Boy, you're just about a cat's whisker from riding down this street on your bike!"

And then it happened, just like Mr. Jefferson had predicted. Tony glided down the street by himself! He screamed with joy, and Mr. Jefferson cheered like he'd just seen a touchdown at the Super Bowl.

To celebrate, Mr. Jefferson ran into his store and brought out a double scoop of ice cream. "A boy ought to have a reward for one of life's big accomplishments!" he said as he presented Tony with the treat.

From that moment forward, Tony loved Mr. Jefferson.

Now Tony raised his head sadly. "Mr. Jefferson, they can't find out who did it. Oh, Mr. Jefferson—they aren't ever gonna find out."

And then, as if the voice came on the wind, he heard Mr. Jefferson's words. "You can do anything you make up your mind to, m'boy."

Tony stood shakily and began to walk toward the market. Could he succeed where the police had failed?

As Tony headed for the market, he gazed at the surrounding buildings carefully. There were stores on either side of the market and apartments all around, too.

Someone might have been looking out the night Mr. Jefferson was killed, Tony reasoned. Someone may have seen something, heard something. Maybe the police didn't ask everybody. Or maybe somebody was just reluctant to talk to the police.

Of course there might not be any witnesses. But Tony wouldn't rest until he'd found out for sure. With new energy, he walked into the liquor store.

When the owner saw him, he snapped, "Hey, boy, you're too young to be coming in here. I know you ain't even seventeen! You want to get me in trouble?"

"No, sir, I don't want any liquor," Tony said. "I'm just asking around the neighborhood about the night Mr. Jefferson was killed. I thought you might've seen something."

"You crazy? You think you're the cops or what?"

"I think somebody saw something and maybe didn't tell the cops," Tony said.

"Get outta here," the man ordered.

Tony shrugged and left the store. At the curb he glanced right and left. The beauty shop next, he decided.

At least they were politer there. "We were closed the night that sweet old man was killed," Elvira, a beauty operator, said.

"You didn't hear anything later that might help the police, huh?"

Elvira smiled and patted Tony on the cheek. "Honey, I try not to see or hear any more than I can help. You know what I mean?"

"Yeah," Tony said. Outside he decided to wait until the next day to do more investigating. The streets were dark and he had to get home.

However, he didn't get home soon enough to satisfy his mother. "Where've you been?" she snapped as he came in.

"I was just talking to some people around the market, Mama. I thought somebody might've seen something and forgot to mention it to the cops."

"Tony Gibbs, I am sick to death of you harping on that old man's murder. He's dead and gone. Now we've got to think about other things. We've got enough of our own troubles."

She reached down and picked up a bundle of envelopes. She shook them as she lectured Tony. "Look at these bills if you want to get mad about something! The gas, the lights, the rent—everybody shoutin' gimme! I work myself to death to keep this house together. But every day, they're throwing more mail bags at me!"

Tony sank into a chair at the kitchen table. "I know, Mama. But it's not right somebody got away with killing Mr. Jefferson."

"Of course it's not right! But you ain't

the police! Sometimes I think you're just like your father. He was always thinking 'bout stuff that wasn't none of his business. Wasn't satisfied doing his job at the mill. No! He had to get together with those other no-accounts and try to open a business. He had no more sense than a mule, but how he'd dream—"

"Mama, maybe it's not right to keep saying 'This can't be done,' and 'That's just a foolish dream.' "

Mrs. Gibbs glared at Tony. "You're saying it's my fault your father ran off? I stepped on all his big dreams? That's poison your grandma put in your head!"

Tony shook his head wearily. "Mama, I'm not blaming you. I know how hard it is for you. It's just that a lot of people don't dream anymore. Look at the ones in the street. They stand around drinking their whiskey, not caring about anything. They've stopped thinking good things might happen."

Then he noticed Shauna was in the doorway, watching in silence. When she saw her brother's gaze, she said, "I believe good things will happen, Tony."

Mrs. Gibbs sighed and tossed the bills back onto the table. "All I know is, my back's hurtin'."

***

The next day after school, Tony stopped at the dry cleaners.

"The cops were in here right after it happened," the woman at the counter growled. "We didn't see anything."

"Sometimes there's drug deals going down at the corner," a girl in back said. "Whenever the old man saw it happening, he'd chase the guy. He just hated the kids to buy that stuff."

"What guy?" Tony asked. "Was it always the same guy?"

"Shut up, Shamica," the woman at the counter ordered. "You don't know what you're talking about."

Tony knew he'd better not pester the girl in front of her boss. So he went outside and waited until she was off work. A while later, a girl came out the front door, pulling her coat around her shoulders.

"Shamica?" Tony called.

She nodded.

"I'm the guy who was asking about the drug dealer. I need to know: did you see him?"

Shamica was a little hesitant. "It was just a dude. He was about your age, maybe. I never saw his face, though. I just saw the old man chasing him away a few times. That's all I know, so don't bother me in the store no more. It'll just get me in trouble with my boss." She hurried away into the darkness.

Tony stared at the corner across the street. It was pitch black because the street light had been broken. He was sure that's why the drug dealer had chosen the corner.

Tony thought over what Shamica had said. It could have happened like that. Mr. Jefferson always worried about the kids. He probably would have hassled the guy and threatened to call the police. Frightened or just plain angry, the guy could have struck Mr. Jefferson and knocked him down.

This corner might be the key, Tony realized. Well, from now on he'd be watching it, waiting for the mystery man to come back.

7 NOBODY CAME THE two nights Tony watched. He began to wonder if the guy had moved to another corner.

The third night he had to study for a history quiz. When he went to class to take the test the next day, he saw Andre enter the room. He looked like a man going to his own execution.

But when Mr. Campbell handed back grades the following class, Andre found he'd passed. In fact, he got a B minus. He'd never received a B on a history test before.

The only A in the class went to Dwight Stokes. Mr. Campbell read from one of Dwight's essay answers, showing the whole class what excellence truly was.

"Here's a young man who takes seriously what I'm trying to tell you," Mr. Campbell said. "Dwight will have no trouble getting scholarships, or doing just about anything he wants."

"Yeah. I'll be long gone from this dump by the time I'm eighteen," Dwight said.

"That's the answer," Mr. Campbell said. "Study, study, then more study!"

"What if you're stupid?" Wayman Townes objected. "I mean, what if you don't have good brains, Mr. Campbell? What if you're just plain dumb?"

Mr. Campbell looked confused. He finally stammered, "Well, any student can—uh, do better and—and improve himself or herself—"

Tony interrupted the teacher's confused reply. "There isn't just one dream, is there, Mr. Campbell? I think there are all kinds of dreams. Everybody can have one.

Tony was shocked by his own voice. But his flood of ideas and emotions couldn't be contained. "Some dreams have to do with the stuff you get from books," he continued. "Other dreams— well, maybe they're about working in a restaurant, learning the business, planning to own the place some day. Or somebody might fool around with engines, dreaming about being a good mechanic.

"See, it's not that any one dream is better than the other. You just find a good dream that fits you and go for it. That's all. It really has nothing to do with what a guy scores on a history test."

Mr. Campbell stared at Tony in amazement. "Why—why, that's well put, Gibbs. You've come up with a very mature philosophy of life."

"It's one of the things Mr. Jefferson told me." Tony looked around the room. "You all remember Mr. Jefferson, don't you? He's the one who paid for the lights on the football field so we could play football at night. He's the one who got murdered, but nobody knows who did it."

There was a long moment of silence. Then Mr. Campbell pulled down the screen and announced that their movie that day was about Thomas Jefferson.

After class, Soroya caught up to Tony. "What you said in class was beautiful, Tony. You should have seen the look on Wayman's face. He smiled. That boy actually smiled!"

Tony nodded.

Soroya suddenly turned shy. "Hey, I've been meaning to ask you something. Well, you know the junior picnic's coming up. And I'm packing a nice lunch—"

Tony smiled at the girl. "Are you asking me, babe?"

"Well, yeah—unless you're going with Michelle. I wouldn't blame her a bit for asking you. All of a sudden I think she sees how fine you are. Fact, she's saying you two will get together one of these days."

"Does she?" Tony said. "Well, I don't know. But I do know I'd like to go with you, Soroya."

"For sure, Tony?" Soroya laughed with joy. "Oh, you are so special!" Then, immediately, she looked sad. "Mr. Jefferson was always saying that, huh?"

"Uh-huh. And he got me to believing it. I used to think I was just another little black kid with a runaway daddy and a mama old before her time. Everywhere I looked, there were other kids just like me. But that fine man taught me there's no such thing as being like everybody else.

Everybody's special."

Tony paused as a rush of memories overcame him. Then he said, "You know, Soroya, when Mrs. Jefferson was alive, she and Mr. Jefferson would do Shakespeare plays in their front room for kids. You ever go to one?"

Soroya shook her head. "I've never been to a Shakespeare play."

"Well, they'd do *Macbeth*. I remember Mrs. Jefferson would be Lady Macbeth. She had a fine, rolling voice. You remember how she'd sing in church?

"Anyway, I remember one speech of Lady Macbeth's. It made me tremble all over. It went like this:

Here's the smell of blood still.
All the perfumes of Arabia will not
sweeten this little hand."

"Oh, Tony, that's something!"

"It means a good, innocent man was murdered. Somebody's hands are stained with blood. And nothing can get the smell of it out."

After school that day, Tony walked the street again, talking to everybody he met. Some were angry he asked questions. Others were afraid of putting themselves at risk talking about a murder. But mostly they were nice. They just didn't know anything helpful.

The next morning at school, when Tony opened his locker, five dead rats spilled out.

Michelle, who was standing nearby, screamed. Zenza Dunne, who also happened to be there, laughed. "Gibbs, you making some bad dude mad?"

"Maybe so," Tony said slowly. His gaze drilled into Zenza. "Maybe you know who that bad dude is, huh?"

"I didn't do the crime, man," Zenza said.

"It's all those questions you've been asking, Tony," Michelle said, clutching her books. "Everybody's talking about it. Everybody is saying 'Hey, what's with the Gibbs boy? He working for the police or what?' "

"I'm trying to find out who killed my friend," Tony said.

"All you'll do is get yourself hurt," Michelle said.

But Tony felt a strange kind of excitement. "Know what this means, Michelle?" he said. "It means somebody around here killed Mr. Jefferson. No big-time drug dealer would put dead rats in my locker. I must be getting closer to the killer, and he's feeling the heat."

Andre came around the corner as Tony began stuffing the rats into a paper sack. "Are those real?" he asked.

"Somebody put them in Tony's locker," Michelle said in a hushed, scared voice.

"Man! You've been nosing around too much," Andre said.

"It's like in that movie *The Godfather.* Remember when they put the horse's head on the guy's bed? It's a warning, Tony," Michelle concluded.

"Yeah," Andre agreed. "Back off, Tony. You can't bring the old man back. So just let it alone."

"You see me running scared, man?" Tony asked grimly.

"I see you dead if you don't watch yourself," Andre said.

Just then Mr. Campbell walked past.

"Somebody put dead rats in Tony's locker, Mr. Campbell," Michelle said.

"That's not a very funny joke," Mr. Campbell said, frowning.

"It wasn't a joke," Andre said. "It was a warning. Tony's getting too close to the dude who killed that old grocer."

Mr. Campbell turned to Tony. "Why are you getting mixed up in this, Gibbs? Seems to me it's a matter for the police. It's bad business when other people try to do the work of the police. It's just bound to cause trouble, even to the school."

"The police need help, Mr. Campbell," Tony said sharply. "Everybody should be using their eyes and ears to help them. Otherwise, it's trouble for the whole neighborhood, you know?"

Mr. Campbell's frown deepened until his brow was like a furrowed field. "Did you get rid of those rats yet? I think I still smell them!"

News of the nasty trick reached home before Tony did. When he walked in the door, Shauna was waiting for him. "Reggie Dunne called and told me about the rats," she said.

"Well, don't tell Mama," Tony said. "It'll just worry her."

"Nothing bad is gonna happen to you, is it?" Shauna's eyes were wide with concern.

Tony patted his little sister on the top of her head. "No way, honey."

He didn't tell her. He didn't tell anyone. But two of the rats in the locker had their throats cut.

8 TONY MADE THE rounds again that night. He rapped on apartment house doors where kids were screaming and crying. He was almost hit by a drunk he awakened.

Before Tony went home for the night, he decided to check the street corner under the broken lamp.

He wearily approached the corner. Then, in a flash, he was all alertness. A dark shadowed figure was standing there.

This was exactly where Shamica, the dry cleaning girl, had seen the drug dealer. Maybe the dealer had come back. Enough time had passed; he probably felt safe again. Now he leaned against the corner of the building, waiting for customers.

Tony approached slowly. He saw, as Shamica had reported, that the dealer was a big kid. He wore an overcoat with a stocking cap pulled down over his ears. It might have been Zenza or Wayman—

Tony crept closer. Then he shouted in astonishment, "Andre!"

Andre almost jumped out of his skin as he whirled to face Tony. "Hey, what're you sneaking up on somebody like that? You almost gave me a heart attack, man!"

Tony grabbed the collar of Andre's coat. "What are you doing here, Andre? Are you selling?"

"Me? You're crazy!" Andre shouted. "I—I just needed to get out of the house, that's all. My old man is blowing off some steam."

"You're shaking like a leaf. Do I have to search you? You aren't selling that junk on this corner, are you?"

"No, man, I swear." Andre saw Tony's grim look and suddenly changed his tune. "All right, okay. I was looking for the guy they said comes here. I needed something for my nerves, man. My old man told me to change the oil in his car and I forgot. Now his engine is screwed up and he's on my case."

Andre looked around wildly. "I don't see the guy. Maybe he doesn't come here anymore."

"You ever *see* the pusher, Andre?" Tony asked.

"No. I was waiting for him one night a couple of months ago. But Jefferson saw me and chased me off. I never saw the guy. But it's somebody from Adams. That's what I hear, anyway."

Tony stared at the boy who'd been his best friend since they were six. Thoughts raced through Tony's head. *Are you the pusher, Andre? Oh Lord, are you the one who knocked Mr. Jefferson down and left him dying in the street?* No, not Andre. It couldn't be Andre.

Tony slowly released his grip on Andre and turned home. Answers were coming at too high a price.

* * *

The junior picnic on Saturday was the one bright spot in Tony's week. As he sat across from Soroya, she began unpacking her basket full of chicken, pecan pie, potato salad, and fruit.

"I have to tell the truth, Tony. My mama helped with a lot with this. Especially the pie. But I made the potato salad," Soroya said.

"You've got a nice mama," Tony said. "And a nice daddy, too."

In fact, Soroya had one of the happiest families on the block. They didn't have more money than the others. However, they didn't squabble all the time, and they were fiercely loyal to each other. Tony hoped that when he had his own family, it would be like that.

After they ate, they lay on the grass watching the clouds float by. "It's beautiful, isn't it, Tony? When you look through the trees, we could be anywhere. We could be in the country where it's nice. Nowhere near these dirty streets."

"Yeah."

"Kids always talk about getting out of this neighborhood. I guess that's because Mr. Campbell is always going on about the suburbs. But you never talk about leaving. How come?"

"When I finish high school, I'll go to the junior college here. They have a great track and field program. Then, if I'm lucky,

I'll go to State. I'm also going to keep working summers at the gym. If I win some medals, well, that'll be great. But I plan to open my own gym someday, right here. I want to do stuff with kids. Last year there was a program where each kid got a piece of sports equipment—maybe a ball or bat. Wow, you should've seen the looks on their faces!"

"That sounds wonderful, Tony. I suppose I'll teach high school math or maybe go to work for some engineering company. I'm not real sure yet."

Soroya looked at the boy lying on the grass, his hands clasped under the back of his head. "You're a handsome dude, Tony Gibbs."

Tony smiled and reached up to touch her smooth cheek. Soroya took his hand in hers, then bent down and kissed him. "I've been wanting to do that for a long time," she said after she sat up again.

"Do you do just about everything you want to?" Tony asked with a grin.

"Just about," she grinned back.

Tony slipped off his junior ring and put

it on the girl's finger.

"You mean it?" Soroya gasped, staring at the little green stone sparkling in the sun.

"You bet, girl." Tony sat up and kissed Soroya back.

* * *

When Tony got home, he didn't hear Shauna singing. She was usually home Saturday afternoon, except when there was a good monster movie showing around the corner. Tony headed back out the door.

She was probably with a couple friends at the movies. It'd be dark before the movie let out, and he didn't want those girls walking home alone. Especially now. Maybe the guy who put the rats in his locker would try to hassle his little sister.

As Tony waited outside the movie theater, he studied the posters. One showed a giant dragonfly breaking loose from a laboratory to terrorize a city. He smiled to himself. This was really Shauna's kind of movie!

When the kids came pouring out, he spotted Shauna and her friends. All of them were still stuffing popcorn into their faces and squealing.

"Did you see when it ate that lady?" one girl moaned, squeezing her eyes shut.

"Did you see its eyes?" Shauna asked. "It had a whole bunch of little yellow eyes!"

Then she saw her brother. "Hi, Tony," she called and quickly trotted over. "Man, you should have seen this movie. It was soooo scary!"

"Yeah, I've been taking in that poster. It looks great," Tony said in a dry voice. "Well, come on. We have to get you girls home before dark when the *real* scary monsters come out."

After Tony walked Shauna's friends home, he and his little sister headed for their building.

"Lot of creeps on the street," Tony mumbled. Just then his eye caught something glistening on top of a three-story apartment building. Something just wasn't right.

Suddenly a shiny round thing came at them. It looked like a flying saucer, but it wasn't.

Tony hurriedly pulled Shauna out of the way. As they dashed for cover into a doorway, a clattering garbage can lid hit the ground where they'd been standing.

"Hey," Shauna said weakly. "What was that all about?"

"Later, Shauna. You just run on home. I'm going up there and see if I can get the dude who threw that."

"Tony, be careful!" Shauna bellowed after him.

Tony ran inside the building and up the stairs. He went two at a time, but he wasn't even out of breath at the top.

At the end of a hallway, he climbed through an open window and dashed up the fire escape to the roof. There he cautiously looked around. But the place seemed deserted. Tony began to think that it might just have been some little kids fooling around.

As he turned to go back down, he suddenly heard something. It'd come from that tiny shed on the roof. Someone must be in there. Tony's hands balled into fists.

9 "COME OUTTA THERE!" Tony yelled. In a second, a boy about eleven appeared.

"Reggie Dunne," Tony said, "what're you doing up here?"

"None of your business, dude," the boy snapped. He was learning to be as tough and arrogant as his brothers.

"You just throw a garbage can lid offa this roof? That's a nasty trick, boy. You could've hurt somebody."

Reggie put his hands on his hips. His dark eyes dared Tony to come closer. "You don't scare me. I ain't scared of nothin'! If you mess with me, you're gonna be one sorry dude."

"I'm not about to mess with you. I just want to know if you threw that lid."

"I didn't do the crime, and I ain't doin' the time," the boy said. Tony shook his head. Reggie was just a miniature version of Zenza.

"Did you see who threw it?"

"I ain't telling," Reggie said.

"Well, it almost hit Shauna. Are you the kinda guy who'd do that to a friend, Reggie? Shauna, she's always been nice to you."

The boy turned his attention to the ground. Finally he mumbled, "I wouldn't do nothin' to hurt Shauna. She's okay. Hey, it was just a dude."

"You recognize him, Reggie?"

"I just seen his back. He was wearing a big coat and a cap. It went real fast. One minute he's here, the next he ain't. I didn't see his face."

"How come you're up here, Reggie?"

Reggie's face suddenly relaxed. " 'Cause I've got pigeons, man. I've got the finest pigeons you ever saw." His eyes glowed with pride.

"Yeah?" Tony drew a little closer. "You got any tumblers?"

"Sure I got tumblers," Reggie said proudly. He showed Tony several which flew up and did a somersault in the air. "I got 'em in blue and green and that orange one there, too. I've got names for all of 'em."

"Yeah? What kind of names?"

Reggie stared at Tony for a moment. "Do you *like* pigeons?"

"Yeah."

"Mama don't. She won't let me have pigeons where we live. She says they're dirty. So I keep 'em here." He picked up one bird. "This one is called Songhay."

"Songhay?" Tony said, smiling. "Where did you get that name?"

"Outta a book. I got a book about old African stuff. So I named my pigeons from the book. I got a pigeon named Sonni Ah and that one is Jenni. This one here is Sonni Baru." He hesitated and then asked again. "You really like pigeons?"

"I sure do. And you've got some nice ones, Reggie."

"Hey, Zenza says you're a creep, but you're okay, Tony."

"Reggie, you sure you don't know who threw that lid?"

The boy shrugged. "He wore a coat like the dudes at Adams wear."

"You know Andre Calder?"

"Sure I know him. His sister went with Zenza."

"Was it Andre?"

Reggie shrugged.

"You mean it could've been Andre?"

"Mighta been." Reggie suddenly darted to another cage and called, "Hey, you seen my blue pigeon?"

Tony followed him and peered at a blue pigeon with ruffled legs. "Real fine, Reggie."

"This blue one is named Hiram."

"How come?"

" 'Cause that old grocer gave him to me, that's why. You weren't the only one he liked, you know. He was one neat old dude."

Tony smiled. "Thanks for the tour, my man," he said. "Later."

He started back down the fire escape, thinking over what Reggie had said. Did Reggie toss the garbage can lid because Zenza told him to? Or was there really another boy? And if there was, did Reggie know him? Tony doubted he'd ever find out anything more from Reggie. There was one rule the Dunnes kept: never, never narc.

Tony made the rounds again that night. He rapped on the last of the apartment doors that had a view of the corner where Mr. Jefferson died.

At one apartment, a small girl answered. "Mama don't want none," she told Tony. She started to close the door, but Tony held it open with his foot.

"I need to talk to your mama or daddy," he said.

Then a young woman appeared, pulling the little girl aside. "What do you want? Are you here about that vacuum cleaner? Listen, I didn't want a vacuum in the first place."

Tony shook his head, wearily beginning the old speech. "I'm trying to help the police find the guy who killed Mr. Jefferson—you know, the grocer. Your windows look out on the street where he died. I was hoping you might've seen something."

"We didn't see a thing. We don't know anything about it," the woman said.

"You see, he was such a good, kind man. I just want to help the police find who killed him," Tony pleaded.

The woman's face softened. "Yes, I know he was a nice man. I know that. But we didn't see anything. I'm real sorry about Mr. Jefferson getting killed. I truly am."

"Eva," came a sandpapery old voice from within the apartment. "Who's that?"

"It's a boy, Mama," the woman called back impatiently.

"What's he saying about Mr. Jefferson?" the old woman asked.

"I'm a friend of his. We were real close," Tony shouted. "I want to help find out who killed him."

"Let the boy come in here, Eva," the old woman said.

"Mama's blind, and she's not right in the head either. You'll be wasting your time talking to her," the young woman warned.

"Please," Tony said, "let me talk to her." His heart was pounding like a war drum.

"Oh, go on then. I don't care." The young woman swung open the door.

Tony walked through the tiny apartment and went into the back bedroom. There he found an old woman sitting with a shawl around her frail shoulders.

"Ma'am, I'm Tony Gibbs," he said gently.

"Why, I know you. You're Hester Gibbs' boy. You used to bring my paper when I lived in my own place. I'm Mrs. Edith Haley."

"Yes, I did, Mrs. Haley. I remember you always gave me cookies for Christmas."

"I had so many friends then. I'm blind now, you know. I don't get out. I'm scared to go alone, and there's nobody to take me."

She fell silent for a moment and softly tapped the arm of her chair. "I miss going to church. You know, Mr. Jefferson always took me to church. Sometimes he'd stop by to read to me. Did you know that? He'd come to visit. And he'd read me the Bible or magazines or something.

"It was so nice. He was the only old friend who remembered me after I wasn't up and about. I just felt sick when I heard about him being killed like that."

"Me too. I—I, uh—loved him very much," Tony said.

"I kept waiting," Mrs. Haley said.

"Waiting?"

"Why, yes. For them to come talk to me about it. The policemen, you know. But they never did come. I tried to get my daughter to take me down to the police station, but she said they'd just laugh at me. She said they didn't care what an old lady might've heard."

Tony could scarcely breathe he was so on edge. "What'd you hear, Mrs. Haley?"

"I heard everything just as clear as a bell. Mr. Jefferson was going to stop by. I was sitting here next to the window, waiting for him to close the market. He always pulled that gate across. I knew when I heard that, he'd be at the door pretty soon."

She stopped and shook her head. "But I never heard that gate close. No, what I heard was Mr. Jefferson shouting. He could get mad sometimes, you know—"

"Yes," Tony said tensely.

"Well, I heard him say, 'Look here, boy, you don't sell dope on my street! No, sir.' And then I heard this boy's voice. I'm sure it was a boy, but it was so mean and hard—"

Tony leaned closer to hear Mrs. Haley's soft voice.

"This boy said, 'Back off, rodent.' That's just exactly what he said. And then—oh!"

The tears rolled down the old woman's cheeks. "I hear a little cry of pain, something like 'ohhhhhh' and then a thud, and the boy running away. Running clean away."

Tony leaned over and gratefully squeezed the woman's hand. It was soft, like satin, though spotted and puckered with age.

"Thank you, Mrs. Haley! Thank you!"

Then Tony ran from the apartment. Everything around him was a blur. He sprinted down the street, startling walkers in his path. He didn't stop until he got to Mrs. Jensen's apartment.

He hammered at the door until Mrs. Jensen opened it.

"Is Dwight home, Mrs. Jensen?" Tony asked.

"Yes, he is. You're Tony Gibbs, aren't

you? I've seen you at school a couple times."

"Yes ma'am. May I see him?"

"Of course. Come in. Dwight's room is the last one down the hall, on the right."

Dwight had a nice, large bedroom. It was much bigger and more comfortable than Tony's.

Dwight sat at his desk with an open text book. He stared at Tony, a little startled. "Well, what're you doing here this time of night?"

"Dwight, I know what you did," Tony said.

Dwight smiled. "What are you talking about, man?"

"I know you deal drugs."

"Well, well. Smart boy, Gibbs. Only a lot of people knew that a long time ago. So what? You can't prove anything."

Dwight laughed. "I don't touch the junk myself. It's just for the poor fools who need a jolt now and then."

"Something else, Dwight—something you overlooked. There was a witness the night you killed Mr. Jefferson," Tony said.

Dwight slowly flipped shut his book.

"Damn," he said very coolly. He looked at Tony. "Does old lady Jensen know yet? And Campbell? He'll pop a blood vessel. So somebody saw me, huh? Well, I'll cop a plea, you know. It never would've happened if the old man hadn't stuck his nose in. Why can't people mind their own business?"

Tony stared at the other boy in disbelief. Dwight was so cool, so calm. No regrets.

A wild rage filled Tony. He crossed the room in one leap and grabbed Dwight's shoulders. "Don't you care that you killed the best man who ever walked these streets?" he cried. *"Don't you care?"*

"He was just an old man!" yelled Dwight, struggling to shake Tony off. "Just a nosy old man!"

Tony wanted to kill Dwight. He wanted to get his hands around his neck and squeeze until Dwight Stokes was no more. He ripped Dwight's shirt open as he grabbed for the boy's throat.

And then Tony saw the burn scars. Dwight's chest was a mass of them.

Dwight laughed at Tony's shock. "Ain't you never seen barbecued meat before, my man? My daddy loved to cook out on me. Hey, don't feel sorry for me, you little punk. Nobody needs to feel sorry for me. I'm going downtown and cop a plea, man. Don't lose any sleep over me. *Because I never lose sleep over anyone.*"

Tony stared into Dwight's brown eyes. They were not full of hate. Nor were they full of cunning. They were simply empty.

The police came quickly. Tony didn't watch them take Dwight away. He just shook hands with Lt. Peters and went home. He couldn't bear to see Dwight smiling and acting like nothing had happened. That terrible, cold smile just wouldn't quit.

Tony realized that Dwight was one of those sociopaths Lt. Peters had talked about. Dwight was a kid who'd only gotten abuse and neglect for most of his childhood. Now, for the rest of his life, he intended to make society pay for that treatment.

***

When Tony got home that night, he wearily told his mother and Shauna what had happened.

"Mercy, that bright boy. What a shame!" Mrs. Gibbs said.

"He was always calling people 'rodents,' " Shauna said. "He even called Mr. Campbell a rodent. It was weird."

Tony couldn't eat dinner. He just wanted to go to bed. He'd thought that once he found out who killed Mr. Jefferson, he'd feel better. He'd thought he'd be able to put it all behind him.

But in a way, he felt worse now. It was as though looking for the murderer had kept him going. Now there was nothing left, just the emptiness. It was over. It was now, finally, over.

Tony lay on his back, a shaft of moonlight streaming through the window onto his face. Finally something broke loose inside and he began to cry. He cried harder than he'd ever cried before.

10 THE TRACK MEET was only a few days away, and Tony was almost dreading it. The time he used to spend with Mr. Jefferson training, he'd spent looking for the killer. He didn't feel in shape.

But that was just an excuse. Basically, Tony didn't feel any real desire to run. There was a big hole in his life, and nobody could say or do the right thing anymore. Nothing could heal his hurt.

"Boy, it's really funny Mister Genius was just a murderer," Andre chuckled. "He always acted better than the rest of us. Now he's gonna rot in jail." All Andre was thinking about was the downfall of an irritating rival.

Zenza and Wayman laughed about it, too. As for Michelle, she kept telling Tony how happy he should be to have solved the crime. And Soroya constantly asked if he was okay now, as if he could shut off all the pain he felt.

None of them understood. They didn't love or need Mr. Jefferson like he did.

On Wednesday after practice, the coach gave him the same old line, too. "Well, Gibbs," he said, "you should be flying high these days, right?"

"I don't know, coach," Tony said.

"What do you mean? You're a hero around here now."

Tony just kept walking. He didn't want to hang around and talk with the coach. He wanted to get home and just be alone.

Tony was nearly off the school grounds when he heard a child yell.

"Heyyy, you gimme that! That's mine, y'big bully!"

Tony turned to see Zenza yanking money from Reggie. "Let loose of the bills, you little freak. Gimme that. I need it! All you'll spend it for is pigeon food anyway!"

Then Zenza spotted Tony. For a second their eyes locked. Reggie saw Tony, too. "Hey, Tony, Zenza's ripping off my paper-route money!"

Tony moved closer. "You mean you'd steal your own little brother's money?"

"Beat it, man," Zenza said, " 'fore I wipe the street up with you."

"I never knew how you got your money before, Zenza. Now I get it. You shake down kids!"

As Tony advanced, Zenza backed up. "Give the kid back his money, man!" Tony snarled. The old cowardice flashed in Zenza's eyes.

Reggie piped in, "You better give me my money, Zenza. Tony got Dwight, and he can get you, too. He's one bad dude, and you better not mess with him!"

Zenza threw down the money. "Go buy your stinking pigeon food, punk!" Then he stalked off, leaving Tony with Reggie.

"Man, you're one tough dude, Tony Gibbs," the boy said as he counted his money to make sure it was all there.

"Well, we pigeon-lovers gotta stick together," Tony said.

"Yeah!" Reggie gave a wide grin. He fell in step beside Tony as Tony walked toward home. "Hey, man, if he messes with me again, can I tell him you'll whup him?"

Tony smiled at the boy. "Yeah."

"And my other brothers, too? I can tell 'em all you're my main man, okay?"

"Yeah, right," Tony agreed.

"Awww-right!" The boy joyfully slapped palms with Tony. "Lotta that old man rubbed off on you, Tony. You got that same look—kinda proud. Like nobody can put you down. Think I'm gonna name my new pigeon after you!"

***

That night Tony had some homework to do for English. But however many times he picked up his book, he couldn't seem to grasp the words. He knew Mrs. Bailey would be furious if he didn't read the story she'd assigned. But he just wasn't in the mood.

At last he slipped the book into his knapsack and headed for the door. "Mama, I think I'll take a walk," he called.

"Tony, how about that stuff you said you had to read for English?" Mrs. Gibbs asked.

"I'm taking the book with me. Maybe I'll read as I walk."

"Boy, I swear, if you ain't getting stranger and stranger!" Mrs. Gibbs grumbled.

Tony ignored the comment and simply added, "I'll be home by ten."

He went downstairs. He thought he might just sit somewhere and read the story. But then he saw Mrs. Haley's third-floor window. She was probably up there all alone. It was too bad she had to lose the only friend she had.

Suddenly Tony set off walking quickly. He didn't stop until he reached Mrs. Haley's apartment.

This time when Eva answered the door, she was much more polite. There had been some newspaper stories about the blind woman who helped solve a murder. A magazine had even paid Mrs. Haley for an interview. Eva recognized they owed their good luck to Tony. So she greeted him warmly and said, "Come in, Tony."

"Is Mrs. Haley up?"

"Oh, yes. We try to get her to go to bed early, but she won't. She just sits there, all dressed up, as if visitors are coming. We try to tell her—" She stopped and shook her head.

Tony nodded and headed into the back bedroom.

"Hello, Mrs. Haley."

"Tony! That you, child?" Mrs. Haley turned eagerly toward the door. "How nice!" A lovely smile spread over the old lady's face.

"Mrs. Haley, I've got a story I need to read for English. It's called 'Door in the Wall,' by H. G. Wells. Maybe, if you don't mind, I could read it to you. Then we could talk about it. It'd sure help me understand it better."

"Oh, I'd be real pleased. I told you how Mr. Jefferson used to read to me, and I did enjoy it so."

Tony pulled up a chair and began to read. " 'One confidential evening, not three months ago, Lionel Wallace—' "

After Tony finished the story, he and Mrs. Haley discussed it. Then as the clock neared ten, Tony stood up to go.

"I had a fine time, tonight, Tony," Mrs. Haley said. "Do drop by and see me whenever you like."

"I'll just do that, Mrs. Haley," Tony promised.

As Tony walked to the door, the old lady's family looked at him as if he were crazy. They couldn't understand. There were some things that only a few people ever understood. Mr. Jefferson was one of those few.

That night seemed to change Tony's mood. He still felt the pain of loss. Yet a little happiness and humor seemed to have returned to his life.

By the time the track meet rolled around on Saturday, Tony was no longer indifferent. He was very nervous, however.

As he did his stretches and warm-up, Zenza and Wayman passed by.

"Well, so you showed up, Gibbs," Zenza said in a taunting voice. "I admire you, I surely do. But what's the point, man? It's just gonna be like the other time. I'm gonna win. You've lost it, friend; you don't got what it takes."

"Yeah," Wayman added, "the magic's

gone. It's like winning streaks and losing streaks. It's written all over you, man, in big letters: *Loser.*"

Both Soroya and Michelle overheard the taunts and stepped to Tony's defense. "Don't mind those bad-mouth dudes," Soroya said crossly.

"That's right," Michelle agreed. She was anxious to join Tony's cheering section. She was sure that, sooner or later, he would come back to her. She knew how good she looked. She felt certain that no boy she wanted could resist her.

"Tony," she said in a soft, whipped-cream voice, "even if you don't win, you're the best guy at Adams. You're ten times better than those creeps." She yelled at Zenza. "Are you listening, Zenza Dunne? I'm talking about you, you creep."

"Hear that ugly dog barking at me, Wayman?" Zenza laughed. "Michelle Calder, I do swear somebody put a curse on you 'cause you're getting as ugly as a dump truck."

Tony turned away from the bickering and stared at the stands. As usual, his mother had been too tired to come to the meet. But Shauna was sitting there faithfully, ready to scream her head off. Soroya was now by her side. She blew Tony a kiss for luck.

Then Tony looked to the place where Mr. Jefferson used to sit. Tony could picture the gentle old man now. He'd have sat perched there, his fine white hair blowing in the wind, his keen eyes following Tony's every move.

The meet announcer startled Tony out of his thoughts. That was his event. Tony moved to the starting line and crouched in readiness. He held his position, left knee poised inches above the ground.

As he waited, all the bad advice he'd ever heard rushed into his mind.

"That's just a foolish dream. You just ain't any good at this. You can't do it."

And then Mr. Jefferson's voice sailed to him on the wind. "You can ride that bike, m'boy. You can, if you make up your mind."

"Get set," came the familiar shout.

Tony was up, both knees raised, hands on the ground, head down.

The shot rang in his ears. Tony was in motion at once. He tore around the track with his usual long stride, his knees up, his arms pumping.

He thought Zenza was close, but he never looked. He never saw Zenza beside him or ahead of him. Tony was alone, running his race by himself. Only as he soared across the finish line did he see how far ahead he'd been all along.

There was silence for a moment. Then the bleachers and the track exploded in applause and cheers. "It's a record, Gibbs!" the coach cried as he ran towards Tony. "Do you know how *fast* you were? You were flying!"

Tony accepted the kisses and hugs from those he knew and even those he didn't. He shook hands and smiled and let people take his picture.

Then they presented Tony with a big, beautiful, gold trophy. He grasped it and held it tightly. Slowly everything and everyone around him seemed to fade. He looked up into the great blue sky as if he were in a trance. Then he held the trophy up, high over his head. The people watching thought he was exulting in his triumph.

But a few, like Shauna and Soroya and a boy named Reggie, understood. They knew that Tony was showing his trophy to a special friend. And, like Tony, they heard the old man clapping as he'd done so many times before. The veined, wrinkled hands making their wonderful music.

For now Tony and his friends knew what to do when a hero dies. You must pick up the fallen torch and run with it.

PASSAGES novels
by Anne Schraff

AN ALIEN SPRING
BRIDGE TO THE MOON
THE DARKEST SECRET
DON'T BLAME THE CHILDREN
THE GHOST BOY
THE HAUNTING OF HAWTHORNE
MAITLAND'S KID
PLEASE DON'T ASK ME TO LOVE YOU
THE POWER OF THE ROSE
THE SHADOW MAN
THE SHINING MARK
A SONG TO SING
SPARROW'S TREASURE
SUMMER OF SHAME
TO SLAY THE DRAGON
THE VANDAL
WHEN A HERO DIES